Emma L. Brock

HAS ALSO WRITTEN AND ILLUSTRATED

Skipping Island
Come On-Along, Fish!
Plug-Horse Derby
Ballet for Mary
Kristie Goes to the Fair
Kristie's Buttercup
Three Ring Circus
Surprise Balloon
Little Duchess: Anne of Brittany
The Birds' Christmas Tree
The Umbrella Man
Uncle Bennie Goes Visiting
Mr. Wren's House
The Topsy-Turvy Family
Here Comes Kristie
A Present for Auntie and Too Fast for John
Heedless Susan
Till Potatoes Grow on Trees
The Pig with a Front Porch
Little Fat Gretchen
One Little Indian Boy
The Greedy Goat
To Market! To Market!
The Runaway Sardine

These are BORZOI BOOKS *for Young People
published by* ALFRED A. KNOPF

PATTY ON HORSEBACK

PATTY ON HORSEBACK

EMMA L. BROCK

ALFRED · A · KNOPF: NEW YORK

19 59

L. C. Catalog card number: 59–12569
© Emma L. Brock, 1959

THIS IS A BORZOI BOOK,
PUBLISHED BY ALFRED A. KNOPF, INC.

FIRST EDITION

CONTENTS

PATTY ON HORSEBACK

A HORSE!

"Of course, dogs are all ri-i-ight," Patty said. "But—"

"You like Yorkie! You're hugging him right now," Beverley said.

Patty was hugging Yorkie. She was hugging him hard.

"Oh, I love Yorkie. He is so cute. But—"

"Then why do you say 'but'?" Beverley asked. "Are his bangs too long again?"

"Well, his bangs are rather long. How can he see through them? But—it's a horse I want. A horse!"

[3]

"Oh," said Beverley. "A horse! Here, give me Yorkie! You can't hug a horse, can you?"

"I could hug his head, couldn't I?"

"Would you hold him in your lap?" Beverley giggled. "And let the rest of him dribble down the steps?"

"Laugh if you want to. I'd hug his head standing, of course. I'd kiss his nose. Then I'd take a long ride. Oh, I wish I had a horse so I could ride. I want to ride and ride and ride!" Her blue eyes were looking far away. "And ri-i-ide!

"I think I'll just get one. I'll start right now to earn

money to buy him. How much would he cost, do you think?"

"Oh, he'd cost money," Beverley said. "Much more than a pedigreed Yorkshire terrier like Yorkie."

"Who's buying a horse?" asked Sam.

He was Beverley's brother. He was a long boy with gangly legs. The legs came up about to his neck. There was only some sweater in between. His hair stood up in long loops. It was worse than Yorkie's.

"I'm the one who's buying a horse," said Patty.

"A real horse? That will set you back some."

"Yes. A real horse—to ride," Patty answered.

"Well, why don't you get a colt?" said Sam. "It would be cheaper, I guess. It would soon grow up, so you could ride."

"But I want to ride right away."

"Oh," said Sam. He was tossing a baseball high up and catching it in his mitt. "Well, good luck," he said. "I've got to meet the fellas."

He gangled off, scuff-scuff.

"Yes, I'll just earn money to buy a horse. I'll start

tomorrow, or even today if I can find a job. Let me know if you hear of any."

"Okay," said Beverley.

Patty was so sudden, she thought. All at once she decided to buy a horse!

"Well, good-by. I must start planning."

"Good-by," Beverley said.

"I'll get a horse, I'll get a horse," Patty sang, "and ride away to the moon!"

That night at dinner Patty only poked at her food. She was thinking too hard to eat.

"Come, eat it up," her father said.

Patty took a large mouthful of mashed potatoes and gravy. Her mind was 'way off somewhere.

"A penny for your thoughts," her father said.

"Oh, I was just thinking, but I could use the penny."

"Oh, thinking," her father said. "Sometimes that's hard work."

"What about?" her mother asked.

"I was thinking about earning money," said Patty.

"But," said her father, "I expect to keep you until you grow up, you know."

"For something special," Patty said.

"Whatever special?" asked her mother.

"For my horse," Patty said. Her eyes were wide with thinking.

"Oh," said her father. He flickered his eyebrows at her mother. "Your horse?"

"Yes, I have to have a horse so I can ride. I think I could earn enough money for it, maybe. How much would it cost?"

"We'll have to look into that, Patty. You could buy a colt for less."

"No, I want a horse, please. A real horse."

"Huh," said her father. "That will require a lot of earning. A lot of work, Patty Perkins."

"Oh, I'll work. I do so want to ride. I have it all planned out. The horse can live in the garage."

"Well, there it is again," said Mr. Perkins. "There's that ordinance about cows and horses."

"Ord—nance?"

[7]

"Yes, a law that they are not permitted to live inside the town limits. But perhaps we could find a
boarding place in the country. So if you want to work
and work hard and work for a long time—a long time,
Patty—"

"Oh, I do!" said Patty. "No work would be too
much. Won't it be fun to ride and ride!" Patty waved
her arms as if she could feel herself galloping along.

"I'll ask around about the price," Mr. Perkins
said. "Then if you want to, you can change your
mind."

"But I won't!"

That night Patty fell asleep counting up money.
It was rather hard because she did not know how far
to count. She fell asleep at $12.50 . . .

She was holding Yorkie in her arms and pushing
back his bangs. The bangs seemed to grow longer by
the minute. She pushed harder and harder. The
bangs slipped back on his neck. Yorkie was growing
bigger too.

"Oh, dear, Yorkie, your face is getting so long!"

[8]

A HORSE!

It grew and grew until it was as long as a horse's head. It was a horse's head with pointed ears and a long nose. It wasn't Yorkie at all. It was her own horse.

So she hopped up on his back and rode away as fast as the wind!

JOBS

Patty was so excited the next day. She danced down to breakfast. She jiggled while she was eating her oatmeal. She joggled while she drank her milk. At last she was going to have a horse. She could ride all up and down every day. After breakfast she helped with the dishes and made her bed. Then she skipped over to see Beverley.

"Yes," she said, "I'm going to earn a horse. It'll take a long time, Dad says. And we can't keep him in town."

"Why?" asked Beverley.

"Oh, there's an ord—, an ord— something, a law about that. Dad knows because he's a lawyer and smart. We'll board him in the country and we can visit him there. But I'll have to work hard to earn him."

"You'll earn him!" Beverley said.

"Oh, isn't it wonderful! Let's go tell Mary."

So they told Mary and Carrie and Jack and Edward. They told their other friends Bob and Johnny and Elsie and Judy and Harold and Margaret and the ice-cream man. They told all their neighbors and the postman too. By the time the sun went down dozens of people knew that Patty was planning to buy a horse. Some of them said that they might be able to help with little jobs. Mrs. Torgenson who lived next door told Patty she would keep her in mind.

"Come over and see me some time," she had said.

Patty could hardly wait to begin to earn the horse. She wanted to know how many jobs she could get and how long would it take to earn enough?

"I'm going over to Mrs. Torgenson's now, Mother," she said after lunch. "I have to begin to earn money."

"All right," her mother said. "Don't be a nuisance."

"Oh, Patty," Mrs. Torgenson laughed, "you're the one and only I've been looking for. Do you have an afternoon off?"

"Why, yes," Patty cried eagerly. "I really do have."

"There's a job I just hate to do. Maybe you won't mind it, and you do want a job."

"Yes, I do," Patty said. "A horse is a big thing to buy."

"Well," Mrs. Torgenson said, "it takes such a long time to pull basting threads. There are a lot of them in these dresses I've sewed up for Selma."

"Oh, they're pretty and I'll be careful. Mother says I do a good job. I pull all of hers."

So Patty clipped bastings and she pulled bastings for Mrs. Torgenson. She was so careful that it took her all afternoon. Mrs. Torgenson gave her lemonade and cookies halfway through. After the job was done, Patty tied the silver she had earned in her handkerchief and tucked it in her pocket. She would not want to lose it.

The next day she washed and dried the breakfast dishes for Mrs. Lane, because she had to rush over to the dentist. A tooth had broken off. She knew she should not have eaten that peanut brittle, Mrs. Lane said.

Patty did some shopping for Mrs. Baker, who had hurt her foot. She took a package down to the post office for old Mrs. Green who did all her walking with a cane. She did a lot of other little things for other people. She tucked the money into a white wool sock and hid it under her mattress. That is what two boys did in a book she had read.

But she wished she could earn it in bigger lumps. She was a little discouraged. It was so slow. It seemed as if it would take the rest of her life at this rate. "It's so slow," she said to Beverley one day.

"Well, earning money is hard, I guess," Beverley said, "unless you have a job. Here, pet Yorkie a little. Maybe you should just get a dog."

"Sure," said Sam, who was on his way out. "I know about some cute puppies on sale for a dollar."

"I do have some dollars," Patty said," but I want a horse."

"Your wants are too big," said Sam.

"Yes," said Patty, "I guess so."

"Well, I've got to meet the fellas. Good luck," said Sam.

Patty went on doing little jobs and earning little bits. It was very slow. The horse was only a shadow.

One day her mother said to her, "Mrs. Helson would like you to sit with the twins tomorrow afternoon. She is going to the city to do some shopping. She'll pay double because there are two of them. I think you're big enough to do it—going on ten. She will put them to bed before she goes."

Patty's eyes were starry. "Things are looking up," she said.

So the next afternoon she crept softly into Mrs. Helson's house next door. It was very quiet with the twins asleep.

"When they wake up," Mrs. Helson whispered, "you give them some milk and graham crackers. That's their little table in the kitchen. Their bibs are tied to the backs of the chairs. They like you, so they'll be good. I told them you were coming. Here are some books in the bookcase for you to read."

Then Mrs. Helson grabbed her handbag and hurried out to catch the bus to the city.

Patty picked out *Freddy the Detective* and began to read. It was so funny. After a while she heard some bawling. You could not call it anything else. A deep bawling and a high bawling. It was Jimmy and Ginny, as sure as anything. Patty ran upstairs and let down the sides of the crib beds. She helped them out.

"I want Mommie!" yelled the twins in one yell.

Patty wished she had another pair of hands to hold over her ears. She stuffed the twins into their overalls and dragged them downstairs. She put them into their

[17]

chairs the little table. They were still howling.

"I want Mommie!"

"Here's your milk and your crackers," Patty said. That should stop the yelling. She tried to look very cheerful. She hummed a little tune.

Ginny took a sip of the milk. Then she dumped the rest on the floor.

"I want Mommie!" she shrieked.

Jimmy took a sip of milk and threw the rest in Patty's face.

"I want Mommie!" he yelled.

Patty wiped the milk from her face with her handkerchief. She twisted her face as she mopped.

"Ho-ho-ho!" laughed Jimmy. Ginny giggled.

"Make another face!" So Patty made another face. And another face and another face.

Jimmy shouted, "Ha-ha-ha!" and slapped his knees. Ginny giggled, "He-he-he!"

"More!" they shouted.

So Patty made all the faces she could think of, and then began over again. Her face ached. Then she stood on her head.

"More!" yelled the twins. "You're funny. More!"

So Patty stood on her head again, and again, and again. The twins did not howl, "I want Mommie," any more. They just shouted, "More, more!"

While she was standing on her head, Patty had an idea. She dropped down on her hands and knees. She took the dishcloth and two dish towels and gave the twins each one.

"Now, we'll wipe up the milk."

They went around on all fours and wiped and

wiped. The kitchen floor was clean. Then they washed the dish towels. Then Patty read them some picture books. Then at last Mrs. Helson came home from shopping. The twins told her how funny Patty was. "And she can read too," they said. Mrs. Helson thanked Patty and gave her three brand-new dollar bills.

"That's the hardest three dollars I ever earned,"

Patty said at dinner. "I think I sprained my jaw too."

"Doing what, may I ask?" her father said.

"Making faces," Patty said. "And I think my back is crooked for good from standing on my head."

"Earning money is sometimes hard work," said Patty's father, winking at her mother.

"Yes," said Patty, "but aren't they beautiful, green and crispy. Folding money!"

She had the bills standing behind her milk glass.

"Just beautiful! Guess I'll go to bed before long. I'm sort of tired."

So the money-earning went on. Every day Patty did some little job for someone. Sometimes her mother had something she wanted done. Her father needed help with weeding the iris bed. There was a little money each day. She hid it away in the sock under her mattress.

"That's some way to bank money," her father grinned. His eyes had teasing things in them.

But Patty thought it was a safe way and easy too. She would not want to run to the bank every day with a few pennies. Patty always knew that her money was safe. The trouble was there was not enough of it. By this time she had some silver and five pieces of folding money. The silver jingled and the new bills rustled. But all together the money was only the beginning of a horse.

One afternoon she was sitting on Beverley's steps playing with Yorkie.

"A dog is a lot of comfort," said Beverley. "Don't you think you should have a dog?"

"A horse would be a bigger comfort," Patty said.

"Well, there's more to a horse, of course," Beverley said. "And you can earn the money okay. I know that."

"I need more money fast," Patty said. "I need more jobs."

"Jobs?" said Sam. He and his baseball were going somewhere. "Huh! Well, how about coming along over to the lot and being the ball-hunter. You know, when the ball flies into Mr. Paine's rose bushes. We'd take up a collection and give you a penny a ball. Mr.

Paine wouldn't chase a girl the way he does us. How about it?"

"No thanks," said Patty.

"Well, it was only an idea. Forget it. I've got to go. The fellas are waiting."

"Thanks just the same!" Patty called after him.

"Now wasn't that a silly idea," Beverley scolded. "They're just afraid of Mr. Paine."

The next day Patty went on with the little jobs. She weeded the garden for Mrs. Across-the-Street Martin. She moved her lawn sprinkler every hour. It was a very hot day and no rain coming. That is the way it went. A little bit at a time. A little trifle at a time. A horse was no trifle.

Patty walked slowly home to her porch and sat down in the porch swing. She kicked a toe on the floor to keep herself swinging. She was tired. It was hot. She held the sticky fifty-cent piece tightly in her hand. Fifty cents! How many of those would she need? The back of her throat ached. Maybe two hundred! Two hundred jobs, maybe three hundred! She swallowed

hard. Then she blew her nose. No, she was not going to cry! But maybe Beverley was right: "Get a dog."

"No! A horse!" said Patty. "A horse. I want to ride!"

She wiped her face hard on her very dirty handkerchief.

THE BIRTHDAY

"Patty, Patty, where are you?" It was Beverley galloping into Patty's yard. "Patty, I have a job for you. Mom thought you might like to do it. We can't because Yorkie doesn't like 'em."

"Do what?" cried Patty. "What doesn't Yorkie like?"

"Cats," gasped Beverley.

"Cats?"

"Yes, Miss Jasper's cats. She's going to see her sick mother. She has to board her cats."

"Here?" asked Patty.

"Yes. She says you're nice and your mother and father too. She'll pay for it."

"Oh," said Patty. "I'll ask Mother."

Mrs. Perkins said yes, if there were only two cats and if they were good cats—trained, you know. And if they would not stay for too long.

So Miss Jasper brought over her two pet cats. Each one had a basket. One was Green Eyes and the other one was Benny. Then she drove off in a hurry to the city to visit her mother.

Benny ran under the davenport as fast as he could.

Green Eyes hopped up into the big chair and began to lick his white fur. He seemed to feel right at home. Benny stayed under the davenport. Once in a while he would peek out from under it for a moment. But if anyone looked at him he disappeared. He would not even come out for his supper. Patty begged and begged. Her mother scolded. When Mr. Perkins came home, he tried too. He got down on his knees beside Patty and her mother.

"Come, puss—come, puss," he said in his deep, rumbly voice.

But Benny stayed where he was. At last Mrs. Perkins put a dish of milk and a saucer of cut-up liver right by the davenport. Later, when they came back from dinner, the dishes were licked clean.

"Is he going to sleep there too?" Patty asked.

"We'll set his basket where he can see it and the sandbox on the front porch," said Patty's mother.

"Just leave the front door open and hook the porch screen," said Mr. Perkins. "Boarders must be treated well, you know," he said with a grin.

The next day Green Eyes ran away. Benny was there all right, under his davenport. But Green Eyes was nowhere to be found. Mrs. Perkins looked upstairs and down. Patty crawled behind all the furniture and poked under the piano and the TV. Mrs. Berger, who was doing the washing, looked all over the basement and inside the clothes-dryer. They were calling in high voices and in low voices. "Kitty, kitty, kitty!" Mr. Perkins was rumbling out in the garage. "Here, puss. Here, puss!" But Green Eyes did not answer.

Then the telephone rang.

"Please answer it, Patty," her mother called. She was on a step-stool looking on a closet shelf.

"Mr. Perkins' residence," said Patty. "Yes, this is Patty. Yes, we once did. Yes, ma'am. Oh, no!" yelled Patty. "He is? Mother, he went home! Oh, yes, we'll be right over for him."

"Don't forget to say thank you," Patty's mother called as she ran downstairs.

"Thanks, thanks so much, and thanks for calling."

[28]

That's what her mother always said, Patty remembered.

It took two minutes or perhaps a bit more for Patty and her mother to run the two blocks to Miss Jasper's house. There on the back steps was Green Eyes saying, *"Mi-e-eauw, mi-e-e-au-ww!"*

After that they kept him on a leash when he was romping in the garden. Sometimes Benny went too, but he did not need a leash. At any moment he was ready to leap back under his davenport.

Two or three days later Miss Jasper came after her cats.

"They look fine," she said. "They look as if they have been happy."

"Oh, they've been happy," Patty said.

"Thanks so very much," said Miss Jasper, "and here is the money for their care and a little bit extra for your horse, because they look so happy."

"Oh, thank you," said Patty. "Thank you very much."

The bills were not fresh and crisp, but they were

green. Patty grinned out loud as she put them with the others. She counted the money carefully. Oh, goody! There was about enough for a quarter of a horse—or maybe for only one fifth of a horse.

"It's coming, it's coming! This is only July. There's a lot to the summer yet. More time to work."

But, oh, she wished she had the horse right now. Wouldn't she have a good ride!

"Earning money is hard work," Patty said at dinnertime. "I never guessed how hard it would be. 'Course I have a quarter of a horse now—or maybe only a fifth. Perhaps I'll have the other three quarters by Christmas!"

"Well," said her father, "how about doing another job for me?"

"Oh, sure!" said Patty.

"Trim around the edges after I have cut the lawn. You know, the edges of the walk and the flower bed. It's a bit of a job, but I'll pay for a good one."

"Are the grass shears sharp?" asked Patty.

"Sharp enough."

So the next day Patty cut at the shaggy edges. She cut with her right hand, then she cut with her left. Then she used both hands. Her hands ached. Her arms ached. There was a blister coming on her right thumb.

"Patty," her mother called. "Don't try to do it all at once! Come on in and cool off. Here's some lemonade."

"Okay," said Patty. She clipped a last clip. Then she clipped her fingers.

Her mother wrapped the clips and the blister up in Band-Aids. Patty ate her dinner that night with fingers sticking out in several directions.

"I'm sort of limping with my fingers," she giggled.

After dinner Patty skipped over to show Beverley her bandages.

"Too bad," her father said to her mother later. They were sitting on the front porch drinking iced coffee. It was a warm evening. "I should have warned her to go easy."

"No real harm was done," her mother said.

[33]

"I do feel sorry for the kid," said her father. "She has her heart set on riding. She has undertaken a big job, earning enough for a horse. She's so determined. Would there be any chance she might turn to a bike?"

"None," answered her mother. "A horse or nothing. She's determined all right. You know her birthday is a week from Thursday. What shall we give her?"

"Something for the horse, maybe, or some money toward the horse."

"No. Something for the horse, I think," said Mrs. Perkins.

"Why not get her the saddle? She'll need a saddle when she begins to do that real riding she wants. It's a big enough job to earn the horse without adding the saddle afterward."

"Fine," said her mother. "That will be fine. Can we manage it all right? I'll postpone that new dress."

"It'll be okay," Mr. Perkins said.

"Won't she love it!"

Soon the ten days had passed and the birthday came. Patty ran home from one of her many errands because there was to be a party. She skipped into the yard singing. She stopped and stared. Then she squealed.

"Oh, whee!"

Her mother and father stood, grinning, beside a brand-new saddle.

"Happy Birthday!" they said.

It was a beautiful saddle, all brown and decorated.

"And a bridle and reins too. It's beautiful! And a sheepskin lining! Oh, oh!" She hugged the saddle. Then she hugged her mother and father. "Thanks. It's so beautiful!"

Patty wriggled herself up on the saddle. She felt very grand.

"It's wonderful! All I need now is the horse to put under it."

Then the party children ran in.

"Oh, look!" they shouted. "A saddle!"

They danced around Patty singing, " 'Happy Birthday to You!' "

Then they gave Patty the presents they had bought. Mary had a tassel for the bridle and John had a bag of oats. Margaret had a bag of apples. Edward brought some old campaign buttons to trim the reins, and Judy had a sack of sugar lumps. Bob brought a bundle of long grass and clover that would dry into delicious hay. Beverley gave her some note paper decorated with little tan and yellow colts.

"Oh, thank you, thank you, everybody! They're

nice. They'll all come in handy when I have the horse. Thanks a million times."

The party laughed and clapped. Then Sam came shuffling into the yard. He had not been invited because he was an older boy.

"Hello," cried Patty. "See my new saddle!"

"Huh," said Sam. "It's swell. Now you'll need your horse. So—" Sam stood on his left foot and then on his right. His face was pink and his ears were red. "Well," he said, "so, the fellas and me, we wanted to help. So here it is. It's just a little."

Sam dug into the pocket of his jeans. He pulled out a handful of small change. He dumped the dimes, nickels, and pennies into Patty's lap.

"Here, good luck," and he went scuffing off.

"Oh, thank you," shouted Patty at his back. "Won't you have some birthday cake?"

"Thanks," called Sam. "I have to meet the fellas."

"Wasn't that sweet of them? You can take some cake home with you, Bev, and Sam can divide it for the boys."

[37]

"Sure," said Beverley. She felt really proud of Sam —for once.

After the cake and ice cream each one of the party had a turn on the saddle and pretending.

"He's a beautiful horse," Mary said.

"Such a lovely color!" said Margaret. She patted where his neck should have been.

"Gidd-ap!" shouted John. "Get going!"

Patty laughed and clapped her hands.

"I can just see him," she giggled. "You're all good riders. Next time we'll have the horse too."

It was a perfect party, everyone said. Patty hung the new saddle on a hook in the garage. She covered it carefully with a big piece of plastic—when she was not looking at it. It was so beautiful!

"I'm only surprised," her father grinned, "that it is not in a glass case in the living room."

THE PRIZE

Two or three days after the party there was a ring at the front door.

"Patty, could you answer that, please. I'm in the middle of my cake."

So Patty skipped to the door and found the postman waiting.

"Hello, Mr. White," she said. "Some special mail or something?"

"Not this time," the postman said, "but I want to tell you what we read in a paper down at the office.

There was a copy of the *Taylor River News*. It told about a contest. The Riding Academy there is holding a contest."

"Yes?" said Patty. Her eyes were shining. She wished he would hurry.

"A contest to win a horse."

"Oh," groaned Patty. "What do you have to do?"

"It's for boys and girls. You answer a question: 'Why do you want to own your own horse?' "

"Oh, boy," squealed Patty. "Oh, boy!"

"Thought you might like to try for it."

"Oh, would I! Thanks, Mr. White. Thanks so much. I'll start in right away on it. Thank you."

Mr. White laughed and handed Patty a magazine and an ad about televisions and things.

"That's all today, I'm afraid. They'll be giving away the horse at a horse show on the first of August at the Academy. So send in your answer, and good luck."

"Oh, thanks. Mother," shrieked Patty. "Mother, they're giving away a horse. They're giving away a horse. They're giving away a horse!"

"Wait a bit," her mother said, "while I put this in the oven. It sounds exciting."

"Oh, it is exciting. The most wonderful thing! I have to say why I want to own my own horse. Why do I want to own my own horse?" Patty wondered. "I want to own my own horse because then I can stop wishing and begin to ride and ride and ride!"

"That sounds good. I'll write it down," her mother said. She wrote it out on the back of a grocery slip. "We'll get it down before we forget it. 'I want to own my own horse because then I can stop wishing'—was that it?"

"Yes," said Patty, "because then I can stop wishing and begin to ride and ride and ride."

"I like that," her mother said.

So that is what Patty sent in to the Riding Academy contest. Her father said it was good and perfectly true, especially the wanting part. Patty carefully wrote it out in big letters on a clean sheet of stationery. She signed her name: *By Patricia Hall Perkins, 10 years old, 620 Dakota Street, New Benton.* Her father mailed it when he went to the office the next morning.

It would be two weeks before the horse show. Patty had never seen such a long two weeks. They went on for days and days.

"It's almost a year!" Patty groaned.

"At least six months," sighed Beverley.

At last, after fourteen days, the two weeks were up. When the day came Patty and Beverley dressed in their new twin plaid dresses. They were blue, so Yorkie had a ribbon to match. Mr. and Mrs. Perkins drove them over to Taylor River. Their friends drove over too, even Mr. White and his wife. It was his day off. They wanted to see Patty win that horse. The Perkins family sat in the front row in the Riding Hall.

The horses were beautiful. The people who had

been learning to ride showed what they could do. They paced and they trotted and they cantered. They even jumped hurdles. Then Mr. Brown, the head of the Academy, led out a somewhat smaller horse.

"How little it is," Patty said.

"It's a gangly cuss," said Mr. Perkins.

The horse had a thin neck and a rib or two.

"Ladies and gentlemen," Mr. Brown shouted. "Boys and girls. This is the colt we are giving away. He is a yearling, going on two years. Too young to ride yet, but he'll grow up fast."

"Oh," groaned Patty. "He's only a colt! I wouldn't want him."

"He'll grow up," Beverley said.

"The best letter," Mr. Brown went on in his biggest voice, "was sent—"

"I don't want him," Patty mumbled.

"From New Benton. This is the letter and a very good letter it is. It reads: 'I want to own my own horse because then I can stop wishing and begin to ride and ride and ride.' "

[45]

Patty's mouth was open, but it did not say anything.

"Yes," said Mr. Brown, "that's the prize letter. It was sent in by Patricia Hall Perkins, ten years old, Six-twenty Dakota Street in New Benton."

Patty's eyes were goggling. Beverley almost dropped Yorkie while she was hugging Patty. Patty's mother and father were laughing and everybody was clapping. Mr. White was standing and waving his arms. There was a shrill whistling. That was Sam and the fellas.

"But I can't ride him," Patty groaned.

"You'll be an old woman by the time you earn the money. This one will grow up before that," said Beverley.

"If Miss Patricia Perkins is in the audience, will she please step forward. We want to present the colt," said Mr. Brown.

Patty just sat there. "I want a horse," she said under her breath.

"Miss Patricia Perkins," Mr. Brown called.

"Patty!" That was her father's voice. It sounded as if he were not smiling.

So Patty teetered out to Mr. Brown.

"Congratulations!" Mr. Brown said. He shook Patty's hand and put the colt's halter rope in it.

Everybody was cheering.

"You don't like colts?" Mr. Brown said. "But the racers in the Kentucky Derby are colts too—three-year-old colts."

"Oh," said Patty. She touched the colt softly on his white face. He nuzzled her neck. He was a sweet horse. She kissed his nose.

"He likes you! Just look at that!" Mr. Brown called out. "Three cheers for Patricia and her horse!"

The crowd cheered.

"You'll be riding by October," Mr. Brown said. "Tell you what. He's too young to ride, but a little sitting won't hurt. That won't bend his back."

Mr. Brown swooped Patty up and set her astride of the colt. Patty gasped.

"Whoa there, old boy," said Mr. Brown.

Patty's eyes were so wide open that probably she would never be able to close them again. She was grinning the widest grin ever seen on a little girl.

"I'm on him!" she whispered. "It's wonderful! And he really belongs to me!"

"Hurrah!" yelled the people. "Hurrah! Hi! Bravo!"

"Take me off. I might stretch his back," Patty said.

"We'll bring him over to your house some time tomorrow," said Mr. Brown. "Around dinnertime, maybe. By the way, what are you going to call him?"

"Oh, I think I'll call him Jim, after my father." Patty's father choked.

"We'll bring Jim over," laughed Mr. Brown.

"Thanks. I'll be waiting," Patty said.

JIM

Patty tried to be happy about winning the colt, but she wanted a horse. She wanted a horse all grown up and ready to ride. She did not want to wait. Next fall was *months* away. But the next afternoon she and Beverley were sitting on the exact edge of the front lawn waiting for him to come. They were munching ginger cookies, Yorkie too. In-between chews they looked up the street.

"Why don't they come?"

At last a car from the Riding Academy came along

pulling a trailer. In the trailer was a horse with a white face. Jim was coming! A few children and grownups were parading after him. The children were cheering as they came. Patty and Beverley hopped up when they saw him coming.

"Here's Jim," they squealed.

Mr. and Mrs. Perkins ran out from the house. Mrs. Perkins was still carrying a cooking spoon. The trailer

stopped by their driveway. Two men from the trailer lowered the ramp at the back of the trailer.

"Don't crowd too close," they shouted.

Then they led Jim prancing down the ramp. They turned him over to Mr. Perkins.

"Better keep him quiet for tonight," one of them said. "He's excited enough now, with the ride and all the shouting. He's feeling skittish. Here's some oats to begin on. He can stay out at night in this warm weather. Mr. Brown told us to tell you that he is broken to bridle and saddle. Not to a rider yet."

"Fine," Mr. Perkins said. "Okay. Thanks for bringing him over."

"Good-by now, young fellow," the man said. He slapped Jim on the shoulder. "Behave yourself. He'll make a good riding horse."

"Thanks a lot," said Mr. Perkins. "We'll look after him."

The crowd stared after the trailer as the men drove away. Then they began to go home.

"Good-by. Don't forget to feed him his oats."

"He'll need water after that ride," someone shouted.

"And a good rub down," called another.

"Looks like a good horse."

"Yes, they're lucky."

"Good-by."

Patty was dancing around like a whirlwind, or maybe two whirlwinds and a cyclone. It was so exciting to own even a colt. Beverley was hugging herself. Wasn't he sweet? Yorkie was barking: *"Yap-yap!"*

Patty's father led Jim around behind the house between the peony bushes and the garden patch. Jim was skipping and dancing. Mr. Perkins tied the halter rope around the clothespole.

"There now, Jim," he said. "You're okay."

"Isn't it a nice yard, Jim?" Patty quavered. "You'll like us."

Jim nodded his head.

"He's really beautiful," Patty said.

Beautiful Jim stepped out with one of his knobbly knees. He bent down his almost-thin neck and nib-

[54]

bled at the grass. Mr. Perkins fixed up a box for his oats. Mrs. Perkins ladled the oats into it with her cooking spoon. Then she scurried into the kitchen for a kettle for water. They had no clean pail. The preserves would have to wait until Jim was through with the kettle. Patty just stared at her new horse. There he was, her own horse. But what a nuisance that he was too young to ride. She wanted to ride at once!

Early the next morning the neighbor children came to call on Jim. There were a dozen or more. They stayed all the morning. Mrs. Perkins made a pitcher of lemonade and some sandwiches for a snack. The children ate them all. When they were not eating, they crowded around Jim. They patted him and rubbed him. They looked in his ears. They would have looked into his mouth too but for those huge teeth. They talked to him and they walked him.

They played he was a cowboy horse.

"Hi, Silver!" they yelled.

Some of them tried to climb up on him.

[56]

"Stop!" Patty shouted. "You'll break his back."

"Behave yourselves or she won't let you play with him any more." Beverley said.

"Come on, Jim," the cowboys said. "How fast can you run?" The boys pulled him and the girls pushed him. Jim did not like all this fuss and push-me pull-you. He stood still.

"Come on, Jim," the cowboys shouted.

But Jim opened his mouth in a big gape. Enough was enough. He stretched out in one long stretch on top of the pansy bed.

"Oh!" the children groaned. "Did we kill him?"

Patty ran to call her mother.

"He can't be killed," her mother said. "Colts can take a lot of exercise." She ran outside. "See, he's breathing. He's just taking a nap."

"Oh," smiled the cowboys. "That's good. We didn't want to kill him."

Then they all crept away home.

"Good-by, Jim," they whispered, waving their hands. "See you tomorrow."

That evening Mr. Perkins gave Jim a good rub down. Patty was kneeling down rubbing Jim's knees. She was smaller than her father and nearer to the knees.

"Now, the job is," her father said, "to find a place in the country where he can stay."

"Not too far away," begged Patty. She was hugging Jim's knees. "I just got him and I have to bring him up so I can ride."

"Yes, not too far away. Then we'll rent a trailer. We can bring him for visits sometimes. And we can visit him there. Now, you are all rubbed down, Jim, and neat as a pin."

Mr. Perkins did find a farmer near town who would board Jim. He did rent a trailer. He did haul Jim out to the Olson farm. Patty felt rather lonesome. Also, she had nothing to do, No more money to earn. She looked at the saddle every morning to be sure it was all right.

She counted the money she had earned. That would help pay for the board at the farm. But perhaps she could keep enough to buy some Mexican boots.

Her father said that boots would be fine and handsome. He thanked her for the help with the board money.

By that time it was Saturday. The family drove out to the Olie Olson farm to bring Jim to town for a visit. They walked over to the pasture where Jim would be. But Jim was not there. Mrs. Olson came running from the house.

"Oh," she panted, all out of breath. "Your colt, he's gone!"

"What!" cried the Perkins family in one voice.

"Yes, he jumped over the fence and left! He's a lively one. Olie's out looking for him now."

"Gone!" It was funny that she felt like crying because the colt was gone. Once she did not want him at all. Now—she could not get along without him. But wasn't he cute to jump.

"Jim's some horse!" Patty said. "Jumping a fence and going off exploring. That's the kind of horse I like!"

"He's been looking since early morning," Mrs. Olson said. "Seems he should be back by now." She looked down the road. "Guess he's coming now. He's just creeping along. Maybe he found the colt."

They all stared at the car coming slowly along the gravel road.

"There he is!" shouted Patty. "There's Jim!"

Jim was snorting and pulling and trying to go the other way.

"Well, here's your colt," said Olie Olson, "and a fine chase I've had. There's nothing so contrary as a runaway colt."

Mr. Perkins and Olie Olson led Jim into the trailer. Jim was snorting. They tied a bag of oats on his head. That hushed him. No more snorts.

Mr. Perkins paid for Jim's board and for the chase.

"Well," said Mr. Perkins as they drove away, "it seems that Jim has no home."

The next day Mr. Perkins asked around town about farmers. He found one who sounded all right and they went to see him. His pasture had a high fence and the gate was strong. His name was Sven Svenson. He was a jolly, big farmer and Jim liked him right away.

"Now you're a fine riding horse," he said, slapping Jim on the shoulder. Jim bounced. Then he put his head on Mr. Svenson's arm.

"I once raised riding horses and broke them in. He'll make a fine horse."

"But he's only a colt and I want to ride him right away," Patty said. She liked Mr. Svenson too.

"Now those two things don't go together," Mr. Svenson laughed. "A colt and riding too soon."

"I know," said Patty, "but I'd 'preciate it if you would make him grow up fast."

Everybody laughed.

"You'll be riding by October," Mr. Svenson said.

"We'll borrow him for a few days now and then," Mr. Perkins said. "And we can visit him here too."

"I wish we could have him at home all the time," Patty said.

"Well," Mr. Svenson said to Patty's father, "ever

thought of moving to the country to live with the colt?"

"Now, that's an idea," said Patty's father. "If the horse can't live in town, you live where the colt can live."

"Well, think about it. Then Miss Patty can look after him herself all the time. She could see to it that he grows up fast."

"Oh, Daddy, could we, couldn't we?" Patty begged.

"How about it, Mary?"

"Oh, James!" she said. She looked a little startled.

"Now, look," said Mr. Svenson. "There's the Hooker place—just off the town limits. It has water and a sewer and electricity. The man who recently bought it is planning to fix it up some. It has been neglected. I'll look into it for you. Okay? It's over on County Road B."

"Good. That will be fine and we'll think it over."

"Daddy!" said Patty. "That would be wonderful!"

So before long the house on County Road B was being repainted and repapered. The barn was white-

washed inside. There was a little pasture near it with a brook and an elm tree. The fence was built stronger and high enough for Jim.

While the fixing was being done, Patty was riding a little along the grassy curbs in town. She and Beverley took turns. They sat on Jim's withers or his rump. That way they would not bend his back. Patty learned how to put on his bridle. Jim did not like it. He champed at the bit. It was in the way.

Sometimes they went out to Mr. Svenson's farm, and Beverley and Yorkie went too. Patty and Beverley took turns riding on the soft country lanes. Sometimes Jim walked slowly. Other times he stepped along fast. Once in a while he almost trotted. Patty would say, "Whoa, there, Jim. It'll jounce your back." Yorkie

always ran along after them on his little legs, saying, "*Yap-yap-yap!*"

The days went by, one by one. All the days of August were gone.

"Oh, botheration!" Patty said one day. "School begins next week."

"I thought you liked school," Patty's mother said.

"Well, I did. Now I don't have time to go. I'm so busy bringing up Jim."

In a few days school had begun. They were still living in town, but they were getting ready to move. Their house in town was sold, so they would soon be moving out to "Jim's house," as they called it.

The nights were growing colder as September passed. Jim came into town only for the day now and then. Usually Patty's father drove her out to the farm, sometimes Beverley too. All day Saturday and Sunday they rode around on Jim. They were using the saddle now. Jim was getting plenty of exercise. He was growing fast. He looked more like a horse every day.

RIDING!

"You know, sometime next month you can really trot," Mr. Svenson said to Patty one day. "We'll have to get Jim some shoes. He can't go barefoot much longer."

"He sounds almost grown up, wearing shoes like a horse," cried Patty. "Isn't it wonderful!"

Soon after the middle of September the family moved out to Jim's house. It was a job cleaning out their old house and moving. It was still a hard job to settle in the new house. Mrs. Perkins was "stand-

[67]

ing on her head" all day. Mr. Perkins was dragging around rugs and shoving furniture. Patty had to climb every day into the school bus to ride to school.

Only Jim had nothing to do but eat. He did plenty of that. He liked his pasture. He scampered over it. He jumped over the little brook. He liked his barn with the manger for oats and the hay in the rack overhead. Jim was happy. He was growing stronger by the minute.

On week ends after that, Patty rode with the new saddle. Some days she rode after school too. She wore her Mexican boots pulled on over her jeans. She felt very grand. She sat straight with her elbows in, just as Mr. Svenson had told her. October came along and she could trot a little now.

Mr. Svenson had told her other things about riding. He told her how to make Jim go faster and more slowly. A little pull on the reins would make him stop. He showed her how to take the bumps in her stirrups when Jim was galloping. She learned a lot and it was so exciting. She did her riding along side roads. It

was wonderful. She had her almost-horse and she was almost riding. Some day she would really ride! "Oh, oh, OH!"

"Keep it up, keep it up." Mr. Svenson said.

After her lessons with Mr. Svenson, Mrs. Svenson would have afternoon tea. At least she would have coffee cake and coffee. Of course, the coffee only stained Patty's milk.

"You know," Mr. Svenson said one day, "you're not bad. You catch on quickly. You'll make a good horsewoman."

"Oh, that sounds grand!" Patty said. "A horse-woman!" Her eyes were shining.

"Would you like to try a longer ride over to the Indian mound someday? It is not too long a ride, but you can see how real riding goes."

"Oh, yes," laughed Patty. "I certainly would!"

"Well, here you are. You ride straight out from your house. Then you turn left at the next road. Then you go past one road and turn right at the crossroads." He was drawing it all out on his paper napkin. "Ride along for a half-mile and turn right again."

Patty hoped she would know when that half-mile was finished.

"Then," said Mr. Svenson, "after about a mile you see the mound. There's a little road leading to it. Not really much to see, but it is one of the burial mounds left by the Indians." He drew a circle for the mound.

"Oh, I'll try it next Saturday," Patty said. "That will be fun."

"If it does not snow," Mr. Svenson grinned.

"It won't snow," Mrs. Svenson said. "Have another piece, Patty."

Patty did.

Patty took the paper napkin carefully home with her. She fastened it to a stiffer piece of paper so it would not tear.

The next Saturday it rained, but the one after that was a beautiful day. It was clear and crisp, the sixth of November. Jim was all skips and capers. He lifted his feet and gritted his new shoes on the crunchy gravel. He trotted briskly around each turn as Mr. Svenson had told her.

"Now for the half-mile. How long is half a mile?

How long is a mile? So how do I know, or you, Jim?"

Jim was trotting along, jiggity-jig. He was feeling gay. He jiggled up and down as much as he jiggled ahead. Wasn't it wonderful! She was almost riding. She was almost riding and riding. Then she made up a poem:

> There was a young lady called Patty,
> She rode on her—her good horse's backy,
>   She rode and she rode
>   And she rode and she rode,
> Then she rode until she was batty.

"There's a road, Jim. Do you think that's it?"

Jim said yes. So they turned right on that road. It was a narrow road with a ditch on each side. It ran between fields of old corn shocks.

"Now about a mile along this road you see the Indian mound. You watch for it, Jim."

"She rode and she rode,

"Then she rode and she rode," sang Patty.

Then they came to a little road leading off somewhere.

"Maybe that's the one that goes to the mound."

So they turned on that road and rode along it. But there was no Indian mound. So they turned again, but still there was no mound. Patty looked all around. There was no pointed mound anywhere. But where was the road she turned off from? Which way should she go?

"I'm lost! Jim, I've lost us! Where is home? I don't know where to go." So they turned again. Jim trotted along the road. Patty pulled on the left rein and turned Jim again. They went a long distance in that direction. Where were they? Patty pulled back on the reins.

"Whoa there, Jim," she said. "Where can we be?"

The back of her throat ached, but she was not going to cry. Jim was tearing at the grass by the roadside.

"Let's go, Jim. We'll have to go somewhere. No use just staying here. I'll go in at the next farmhouse and ask how to get home. Let's go, Jim."

She urged him to go on. So Jim lifted his head and started off. Then he stopped with a jerk. He stopped

so suddenly that Patty almost fell. Then he blew a big breath. He turned around and stepped off in the direction from which they had been coming. That bit of grass had given him an appetite. He would like some oats and hay or even a whole pasture.

"I can't steer you," Patty said. "I don't know where we are!" No, she must not try to talk. It was harder to keep from crying when she talked.

Jim stepped along faster. He turned one corner, then he turned another and another. Here was a good gravel road. Jim began to trot. He held his head high and trotted along. Then he ran faster.

"I do wish I knew where we are!"

Jim whinnied and ran faster yet.

"Here's a farm, Jim," Patty said. "Let's turn in here, Jim, and ask the way home."

She pulled on the left rein, but Jim did not turn.

"Jim! Did you hear me? Turn."

But Jim leaped on. His nostrils were spread. His ears were pointed forward. He was breathing hard. His new shoes made loud crunches on the gravel. He

galloped. He galloped fast, as fast as the wind. Patty took the bounces in her stirrups. Her hair blew out straight behind her.

She was really riding now. Really riding! But she did wish she knew where she was going in such a hurry. Wow! Really-riding was rough. She could hardly stay in the saddle. Wasn't it fun! She was riding, riding, riding, faster than the wind, faster even than a hurricane! Maybe to the moon! Wasn't it wonderful!

"I don't care where I am or where I'm going!" shouted Patty. "I'm ri-i-iding!"

Jim gave a loud whinny and whirled into a side road that led to a farm.

"Why!" gasped Patty. "It's Mr. Svenson's. How did we ever get here?"

There was Mr. Svenson coming to welcome her.

"Well now," he said, "were you looking for the Indian mound?"

"Yes, and I got lost. Jim brought me here."

Jim whinnied and walked toward the barn. He was blowing hard. His coat was dark with sweat.

"You know what?" Mr. Svenson laughed. "He's lived here so much that he thinks this is home. Horses always find their way back to their food. All right, Jim, I'll get you your oats and we'll rub you down. You certainly are hot."

"Isn't he smart though," Patty said. "Imagine his being that smart. I was lost, but Jim wasn't. Isn't he wonderful!"

"Oh, he's a fine horse," Mr. Svenson said, "and he can certainly go."

"Yes, didn't we ride though! I didn't know it would be that fast—real riding. Was that real riding, Mr. Svenson?"

"That," said Mr. Svenson, "was real riding. You came along the road lickity-larrup. And there you stuck on the saddle, right tight in the saddle. It was great. Great riding it was, and on a fine horse."

"Oh," squealed Patty.

"Miss Patricia Perkins," Mr. Svenson said soberly. "Miss Patricia Perkins, I hereby give you a diploma as a horsewoman!"

"Oh, my!" gasped Patty. "A horsewoman!"

RIDING!

Patty's eyes were very blue and filled with stars. Her smile would probably be there the rest of her life.

"A horsewoman! I must call Bev and tell her. A real horsewoman!"

About the Author

Miss Brock received a B.A. degree at the University of Minnesota, where she majored in English and writing. She had further study at the Minneapolis School of Art and the Art Students League in New York with periods of work in the Minneapolis Public Library Art Department and in the Children's Room of the New York Public Library. She has travelled many times to New York and to Europe to study and collect material for picture books. Miss Brock lives in Minneapolis, Minnesota, and has written and illustrated over twenty-five Borzoi Books for Young People.

A NOTE ON THE TYPE

The text of this book was set on the Linotype in Basker-ville, a facsimile of the type designed by John Baskerville, Birmingham, England, in 1754. The original Basker-ville type was one of the forerunners of the "modern" style of type faces. The Linotype copy was cut under the supervision of George W. Jones of London.

The book was composed, printed, and bound by *H. Wolff*, New York.